Disney

BEAUTY and the BEAST

Ladybird Books

Once upon a time, in a faraway land, a handsome young prince lived in a beautiful castle.

The Prince had everything he could wish for, but he was spoiled and selfish. When an old beggar woman came to the castle one cold night, seeking shelter, he sneered at her ugliness and sent her away.

The old woman, who was really an enchantress, decided to teach the Prince a lesson. She turned him into a hideous beast and cast a spell on the castle and everyone in it.

But she left two gifts for the Prince: a magic mirror, which was to be his only view of the outside world, and an enchanted rose. The rose would bloom until the Prince's twenty-first year. If by then he could learn to love another, and win that person's love, the Enchantress's spell would be broken. If not, he would remain a beast for ever.

In a little village near the castle, a lovely young girl named Belle lived with her father Maurice, an inventor. Belle was kind and gentle, and loved to read stories of kings and princes.

Belle was also very beautiful. She was so beautiful that Gaston, the handsomest and most conceited man in the village, decided she was the only girl worthy of him. But when Gaston asked Belle to marry him, she refused. He was far too vain and arrogant for her.

One afternoon, Belle's father set off on his faithful horse Philippe to take his latest invention to a fair. As they travelled through the forest, a cold fog descended, and soon they were lost.

Suddenly Maurice and Philippe heard wolves howling. Philippe was terrified and reared up, throwing Maurice to the ground. In a panic, the horse fled. Maurice had to struggle through the mist on his own, chased by the hungry wolves. He stumbled down a hill and found himself in front of a huge, forbidding castle. Thinking he might be safe there, he pushed open the heavy iron gate and rushed inside.

To his amazement, Maurice was greeted by a group of very excited enchanted objects! There were Lumiere the candelabra, Cogsworth the clock, and Mrs Potts the teapot with her son, Chip. They were all eager to help Maurice, but they were worried about what their master would say — he never allowed guests in the castle.

Just as they feared, their master, the Beast, was furious when he saw Maurice. "Strangers are not welcome here!" he thundered, dragging Maurice off to a dungeon.

When Philippe arrived home all alone, Belle knew that something must have happened to her father. "Take me to Papa, Philippe," she said, climbing onto the horse's back.

Though he was exhausted, the faithful Philippe obediently took Belle back through the forest to the Beast's castle.

"Papa? Papa? Where are you?" called Belle, wandering through the castle's vast, echoing corridors. At last she found Maurice, frightened and shivering in his tiny cell. "Oh, Papa!" she cried. "We must get you out of here!"

"He is my prisoner!" bellowed a voice above her. Cowering in fear, Belle turned to see the Beast looming above her. Though she was terrified, she bravely said, "Please let him go. You can take me in his place."

"All right," said the Beast. "But you must promise to stay here for ever."

Belle agreed, and her father was set free.

The Beast insisted that Belle should join him for dinner. "I'm not hungry!" she retorted, angrily.

"If you won't eat with me," thundered the Beast, "then you won't eat at all!"

But later that night the enchanted objects took pity on Belle and served her a dazzling supper. Afterwards, they took her on a tour of the castle.

The Beast had forbidden Belle to go to the West Wing, where his lair was, but she was curious to see what was there. When Cogsworth's back was turned, she crept away to explore by herself.

Belle was shocked at the state of the Beast's room. It was filthy and strewn with torn clothes and broken furniture. The only beautiful thing in it was the enchanted rose, blooming under a glass jar. As Belle reached out to touch it, the Beast burst in, enraged.

"How dare you come in here!" he roared. "Get out at once!" Belle was terrified. Despite her promise to stay, she fled into the snowy night.

Belle and Philippe sped away from the castle into the dark, misty forest. But before they got very far, they were attacked by ferocious wolves. Just as it seemed that they were doomed, a mighty roar filled the air. The Beast had come to rescue Belle. He set upon the wolves with all his strength, and there was a terrible battle. But the wolves were no match for the Beast. Whining, they limped away in defeat.

When Belle saw that the Beast was injured, she led him back to the castle and tended to his wounds. It was the beginning of a warm friendship between them.

But Belle missed her father. "You can see him in my magic mirror," said the Beast. "It will show you anything you want."

When she looked in the mirror, Belle was shocked to see her father, cold and sick, lost in the forest as he searched for her.

"I must help him!" she cried.

The Beast couldn't bear to see Belle unhappy. Even though he knew that she was his last chance to break the spell, he had to release her. "Go to him," he said. "But take the mirror, so you can remember me."

The mirror guided Belle to her father, and she took him home, where she nursed him back to health.

"I can't believe that Beast let you go," said Maurice to Belle one morning.

"He's different now, Papa," said Belle. "He's changed."

Just then there was a knock on the door. It was Gaston, with a crowd of villagers and the director of the Insane Asylum.

"If you don't marry me, I'll have your father locked up," Gaston threatened. "The old man's mad! He's been raving about a horrible Beast keeping you prisoner in a castle!"

"My father's not crazy!" shouted Belle. "The Beast is real. See for yourselves!" And she held up the magic mirror.

Gaston, angry that his plan had failed, grabbed the mirror. "This Beast will steal your children!" he shouted to the villagers. "He's a danger to us all. I say we kill him!"

Shouts of: "Kill the Beast!" rose from the crowd, and the villagers ran home to get weapons and torches.

The angry mob, guided by the magic mirror, stormed the castle.

Since Belle had left, the Beast had been too sad and lonely to care about anything, so when Gaston forced him out of his lair onto the castle roof, he didn't put up much of a fight. Only when he heard Belle's voice did he look up and run towards her.

As soon as the Beast's back was turned, Gaston saw his chance. He drew his dagger and stabbed the Beast in the back.

With a howl of pain, the Beast turned on his attacker. Trying to escape, Gaston tripped and fell over the edge of the roof.

But it was too late. The Beast collapsed.

"Don't die!" sobbed Belle, leaning over to kiss the Beast. "I love you!"

Suddenly the air around them shimmered with a magic mist, and the Beast opened his eyes. Before Belle's astonished gaze, the Beast began to change into a handsome young man.

Belle couldn't understand what was going on, until the Prince said, "Belle, it's me." The magic in the air carried Belle and the Prince into the ballroom, where they danced to a beautiful love song. The enchanted objects gathered round them and, one by one, they changed back into the happy, devoted servants they once had been. The Prince had learned to love unselfishly, and the spell that had kept him prisoner for so long was finally broken.

First edition

Published by Ladybird Books Ltd Loughborough Leicestershire UK

Printed in England (3)